きつね と つる
イソップ どうわ

The Fox and the Crane
An Aesop's Fable

retold by Dawn Casey

illustrated by Jago

Japanese translation by Maiko Osada

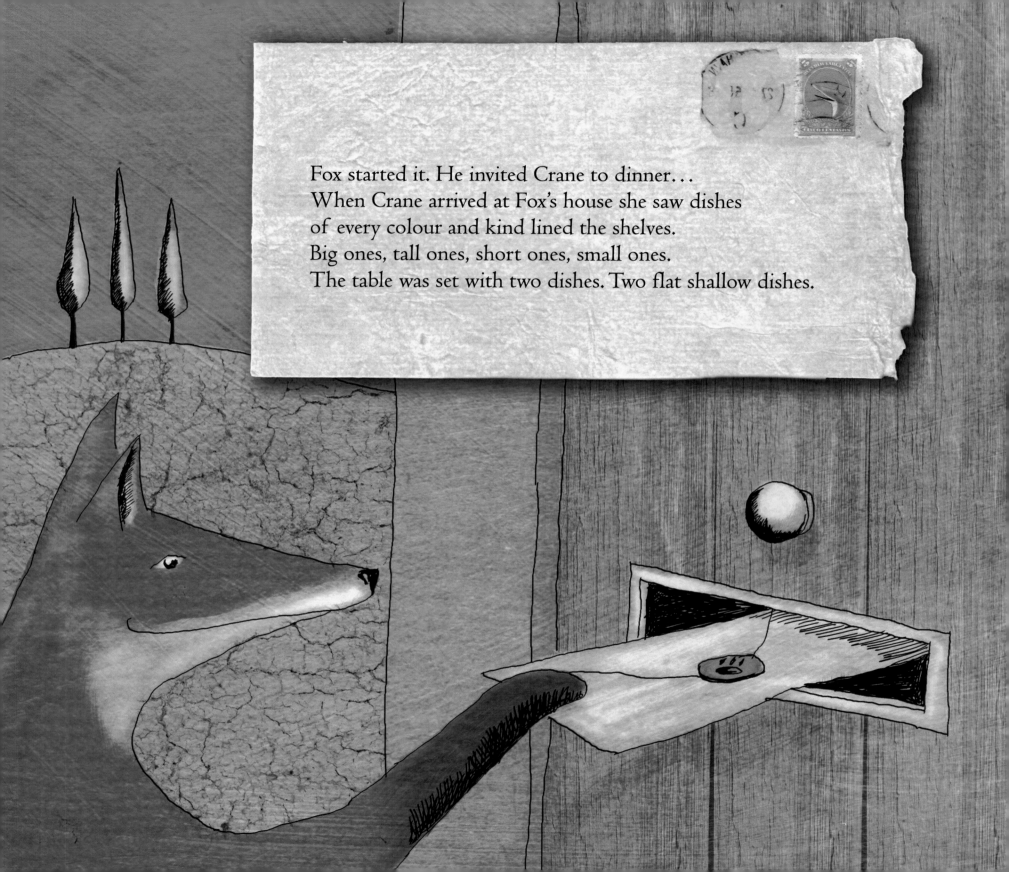

Fox started it. He invited Crane to dinner...
When Crane arrived at Fox's house she saw dishes
of every colour and kind lined the shelves.
Big ones, tall ones, short ones, small ones.
The table was set with two dishes. Two flat shallow dishes.

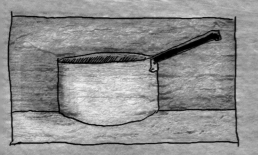

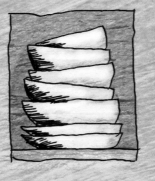

きつねが　さきに　はじめたのです。きつねは　つるを　ゆうしょくに
しょうたいしたのですが...
つるは　きつねの　いえで　いろいろな　いろや　しゅるいの
おさらが　たなに　ならんでいるのを　みました。おおきいもの、
せのたかいもの、みじかいもの、ちいさいもの。テーブルには
ふたつの　おさらが　おいてありました。
あさく　ひらべったい　にまいの　おさらです。

つるは　ほそながい　くちばしで　おさらを　つつきました。しかし　どんなに
いっしょうけんめいに　がんばっても　ひとくちも　スープを　のめません。

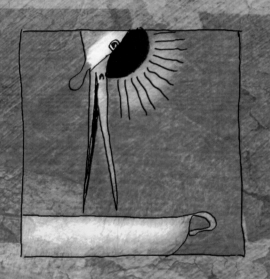  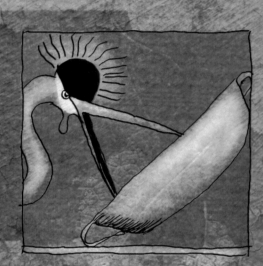

Crane pecked and she picked with her long thin beak. But no matter
how hard she tried she could not get even a sip of the soup.

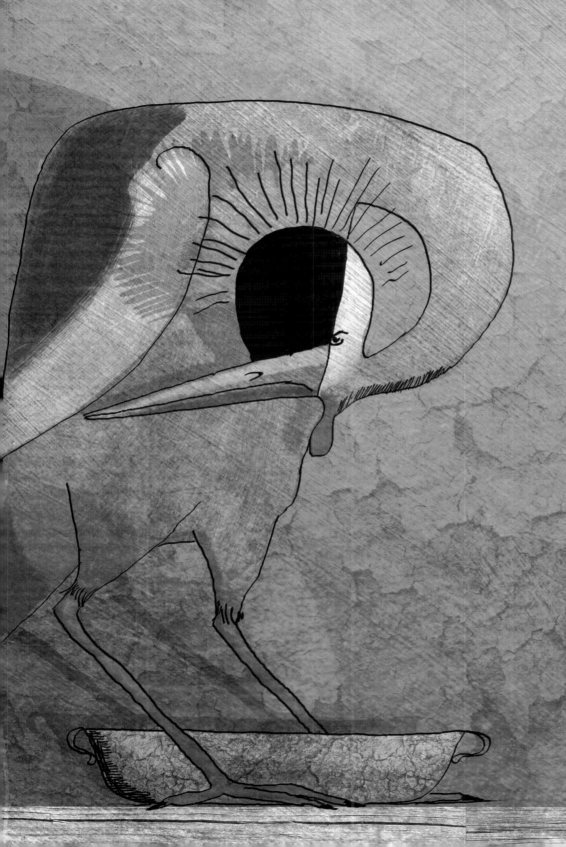

きつねは　いっしょうけんめいに
がんばっている　つるを　みて
くすくすと　わらいました。
きつねは　スープに　したを
つけると　ピチャピチャと　なめ
そして　いっきに　のみほしました。

Fox watched Crane struggling and sniggered.
He lifted his own soup to his lips, and with
a SIP, SLOP, SLURP he lapped it all up.
"Ahhhh, delicious!" he scoffed, wiping his
whiskers with the back of his paw.
"Oh Crane, you haven't touched your soup,"
said Fox with a smirk. "I AM sorry you
didn't like it," he added, trying not to snort
with laughter.

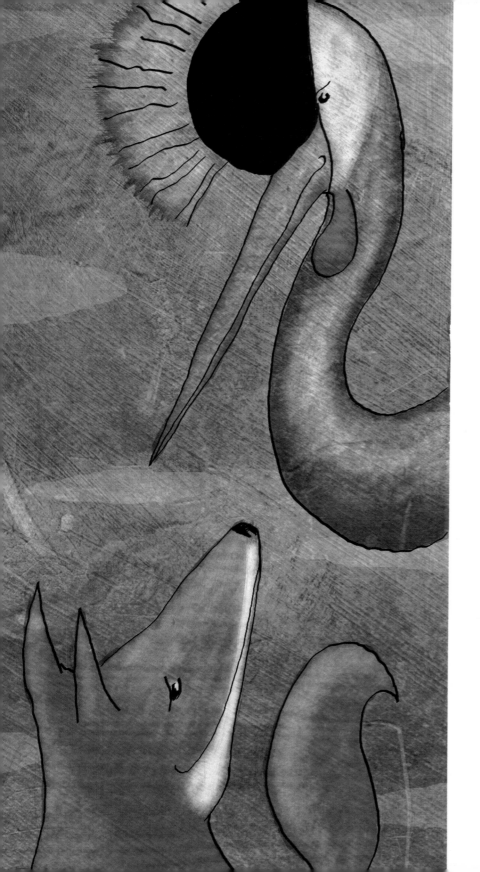

つるは　なにも　いいませんでした。つるは
スープをみつめ　おさらを　みつめ
そして　きつねを　みつめ　ほほえみました。
「きつねさん、やさしい　おもてなしを
ありがとう。きょうの　おれいを　したいの。
ぜひ　わたしの　うちにも　しょくじに
きてください。」

きつねが　つるのうちに　ついたとき　まどから
おいしそうな　においが　ただよっていました。
きつねは　はなを　ひくひく　させました。
くちの　なかは　よだれで　いっぱいです。
おなかが　ゴロゴロ　なりました。きつねは
くちを　なめました。

Crane said nothing. She looked at the meal. She looked
at the dish. She looked at Fox, and smiled.
"Dear Fox, thank you for your kindness," said Crane
politely. "Please let me repay you – come to dinner at
my house."

When Fox arrived the window was open. A delicious
smell drifted out. Fox lifted his snout and sniffed. His
mouth watered. His stomach rumbled. He licked his lips.

「きつねさん、さあ、
おはいりください。」と　つるは
はねを　ゆうがに　ひろげながら
いいました。
きつねは　つるを　おしのけて
はいりました。たなには
いろいろな　いろと　しゅるいの
おさらが　おいてあります。
あかいもの、あおいもの、
ふるいもの、あたらしいもの。
テーブルには　ふたつの
おさらが　おいてありました。
ふたつの　ほそながい　つぼでした。

"My dear Fox, do come in," said Crane,
extending her wing graciously.
Fox pushed past. He saw dishes of
every colour and kind lined the shelves.
Red ones, blue ones, old ones, new ones.
The table was set with two dishes.
Two tall narrow dishes.

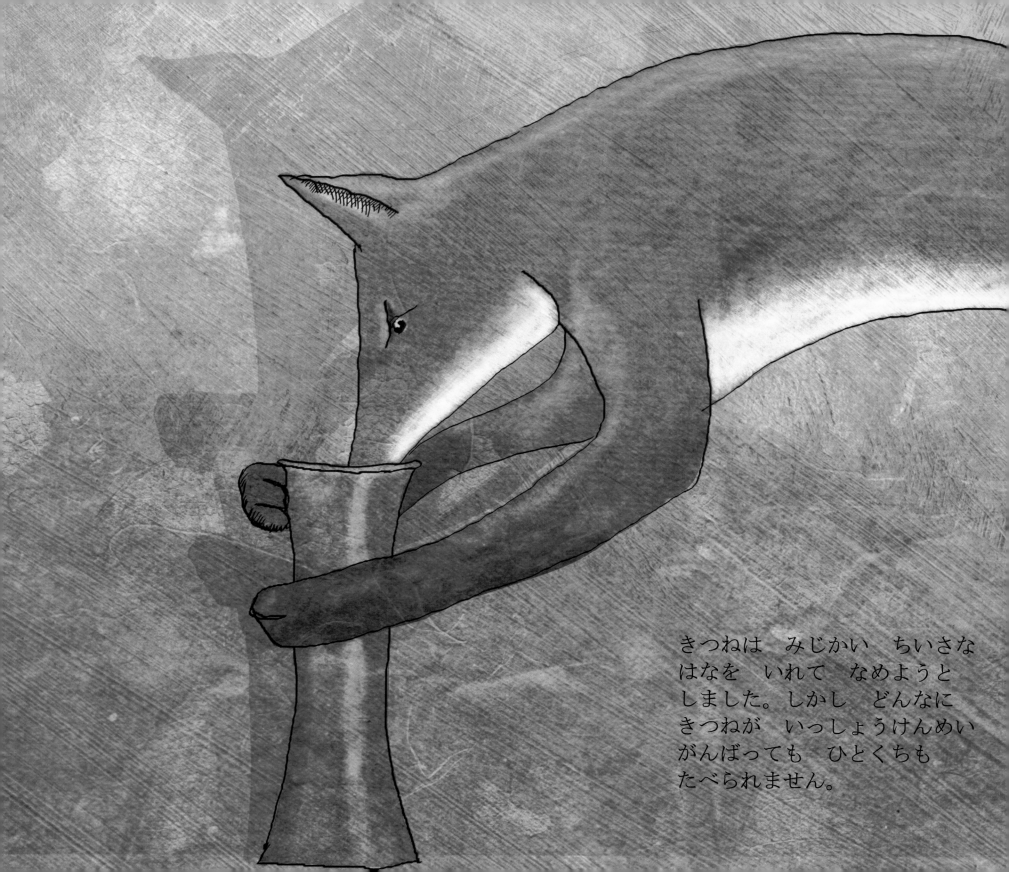

きつねは　みじかい　ちいさな
はなを　いれて　なめようと
しました。しかし　どんなに
きつねが　いっしょうけんめい
がんばっても　ひとくちも
たべられません。

Fox licked and he lapped with his short little snout.
But no matter how hard he tried he could not
get even a mouthful of the meal.

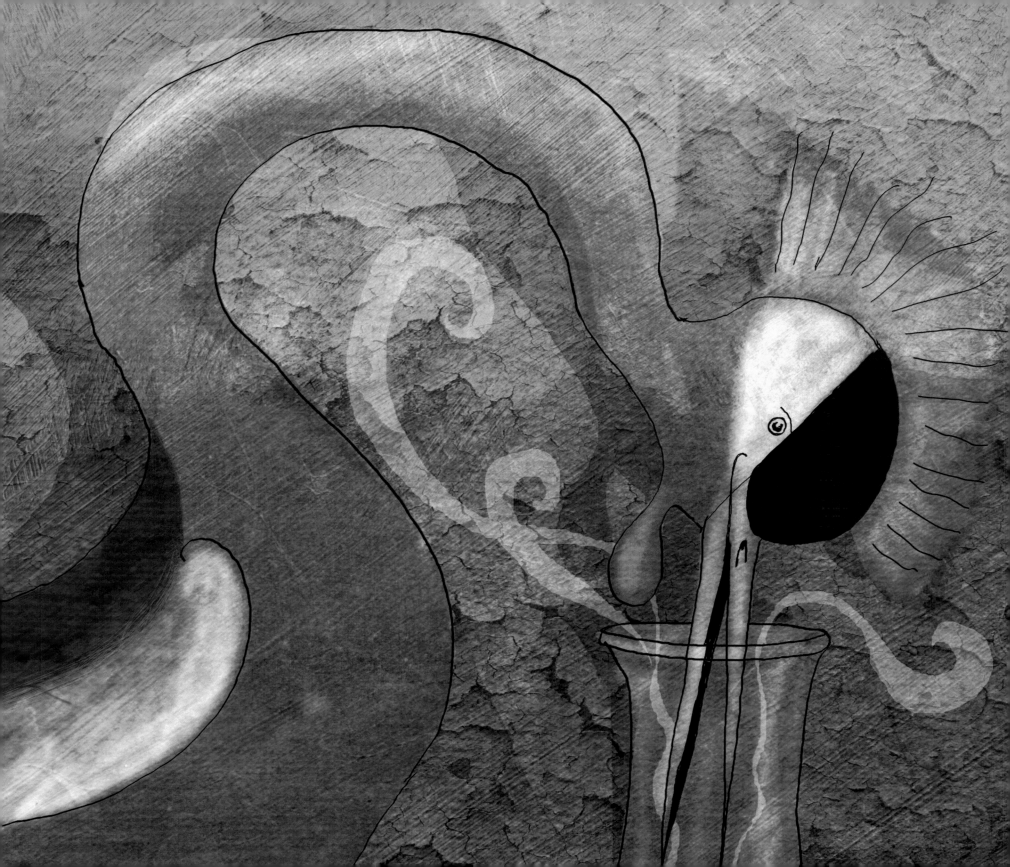

つるは　ゆっくりと　ひとくちづつ　あじわいながら　たべました。
「きつねさん、きょうは　きてくださって　ありがとう。」と
つるは　ほほえみました。「この　あいだの　おれいが　できて
とても　うれしいわ。」

きつねの　おなかが　ゴロゴロと　なりました。
きつねは　おなかを　すかせたまま　いえに　かえりました。

Crane ate her meal very slowly, savouring every mouthful.
"Dear Fox, thank you so much for coming," she smiled,
"it has been a pleasure to repay your kindness."

Fox's tummy gurgled and grumbled.
And when he went home, he was still hungry.

The Fox and the Crane

Writing Activity:
Read the story. Explain that we can write our own fable by changing the characters.

Discuss the different animals you could use, bearing in mind what different kinds of dishes they would need! For example, instead of the fox and the crane you could have a tiny mouse and a tall giraffe.

Write an example together as a class, then give the children the opportunity to write their own. Children who need support could be provided with a writing frame.

Art Activity:
Dishes of every colour and kind! Create them from clay, salt dough, play dough… Make them, paint them, decorate them…

Maths Activity:
Provide a variety of vessels: bowls, jugs, vases, mugs… Children can use these to investigate capacity:

Compare the containers and order them from smallest to largest.

Estimate the capacity of each container.

Young children can use non-standard measures e.g. 'about 3 beakers full'.

Check estimates by filling the container with coloured liquid ('soup') or dry lentils.

Older children can use standard measures such as a litre jug, and measure using litres and millilitres. How near were the estimates?

Label each vessel with its capacity.

The King of the Forest

Writing Activity:
Children can write their own fables by changing the setting of this story. Think about what kinds of animals you would find in a different setting. For example how about 'The King of the Arctic' starring an arctic fox and a polar bear!

Storytelling Activity:
Draw a long path down a roll of paper showing the route Fox took through the forest. The children can add their own details, drawing in the various scenes and re-telling the story orally with model animals.

If you are feeling ambitious you could chalk the path onto the playground so that children can act out the story using appropriate noises and movements! (They could even make masks to wear, decorated with feathers, woollen fur, sequin scales etc.)

Music Activity:
Children choose a forest animal. Then select an instrument that will make a sound that matches the way their animal looks and moves. Encourage children to think about musical features such as volume, pitch and rhythm. For example a loud, low, plodding rhythm played on a drum could represent an elephant.

Children perform their animal sounds. Can the class guess the animal?

Children can play their pieces in groups, to create a forest soundscape.

もりの　おうさま

中国ぐうわ

The King of the Forest

A Chinese Fable

retold by Dawn Casey

illustrated by Jago

Japanese translation by Maiko Osada

きつねが　もりを　あるいていると　くさむらの
なかで　なにかが　うごきました。
ざわざわ　　　　なにか　おおきいもの。
ぱちくり　　　　きいろい　め。
ぴかぴか　　　　ナイフのように　とがった　は。

Fox was walking in the forest when he heard something moving
in the long grass.
RUSTLE   Something big.
BLINK   Something with yellow eyes.
FLASH   Something with teeth like knives.

「おはよう、かわいい　きつねくん。」と　とらは　にやりと　わらいました。
ナイフのように　とがった　はが　みえます。
きつねは　はっとして　いきを　のみこみました。
「あえて　うれしいよ。」と　とらは　ゴロゴロと　のどを　ならしました。
「ちょうど　おなかがすいてきた　ところだったんだ。」
きつねは　いそいで　かんがえました。「おろかもの！」と　きつねは　いいました。
「わたしが　もりの　おうさまだと　いうことを　しらないのか？」
「おまえが、もりの　おうさまだと？」と　とらは　おおきな　こえで　わらいました。
「しんじられないのなら、」と　きつねは　どうどうと　いいました。「わたしのうしろを
あるけば　わかる。わたしが　どれほど　みなに　おそれられているかが。」
「おもしろい。」と　とらは　いいました。
そこで　きつねは　ぶらぶらと　あるきはじめました。とらは　しっぽを　ピンと
のばして　おおいばりで　あとを　ついていきました。すると…

"Good morning little fox," Tiger grinned, and his mouth was nothing but teeth.
Fox gulped.
"I am pleased to meet you," Tiger purred. "I was just beginning to feel hungry."
Fox thought fast. "How dare you!" he said. "Don't you know I'm the King of the Forest?"
"You! King of the Forest?" said Tiger, and he roared with laughter.
"If you don't believe me," replied Fox with dignity, "walk behind me and you'll see —
everyone is scared of me."
"This I've got to see," said Tiger.
So Fox strolled through the forest. Tiger followed behind proudly, with his tail held high,
until…

ガーガー！
かぎのように　まがった　おおきな　くちばしの
たかです！　しかし、たかは　とらを　ちらっと
みると　そのまま　はやしの　ほうに　はばたいて
いってしまいました。
「わかったか？」と　きつねが　いいました。
「みな　わたしを　おそれているのだ！」
「しんじられん！」と　とらが　いいました。

SQUAWK!
A huge hook-beaked hawk! But the hawk took
one look at Tiger and flapped into the trees.
"See?" said Fox. "Everyone is scared of me!"
"Unbelievable!" said Tiger.
　　　　　Fox strode on through the forest.
　　　　　Tiger followed behind lightly,
　　　　　with his tail drooping slightly,
　　　　　until…

がぉー！
おおきな　くろい　くまです！　しかし　くまは　とらを
ちらっと　みると　しげみのほうに　はしって　いきました。
「わかったか？」と　きつねが　いいました。
「みな　わたしを　おそれているのだ！」
「まさか！」と　とらが　いいました。
きつねは　ぶらぶらと　また　あるきはじめました。
とらは　しっぽを　じめんに　たらしながら
おとなしく　あとを　ついていきました。
すると...

GROWL!
A big black bear! But the bear took one look
at Tiger and crashed into the bushes.
"See?" said Fox. "Everyone is scared of me!"
"Incredible!" said Tiger.
Fox marched on through the forest. Tiger
followed behind meekly, with his tail
dragging on the forest floor, until...

シュー！
こそこそした　スルスルの　へびです！ところが
へびは　とらを　ちらっと　みると　やぶのなかに
きえていきました。
「わかったか？」と　きつねが　いいました。
「みな　わたしを　おそれているのだ！」

HISSSSSSS!
A slinky slidey snake! But the snake took one look
at Tiger and slithered into the undergrowth.
"SEE?" said Fox. "EVERYONE IS SCARED
OF ME!"

「わかりました。あなたは　もりの　おうさま、そして　わたしは
あなたの　けらいです。」と　とらが　いいました。
「よし！」と　きつねは　いいました。「では、いきなさい！」

しっぽを　たらしながら　とらは　にげていきました。

"I do see," said Tiger, "you are the King of the Forest and I am your humble servant."
"Good," said Fox. "Then, be gone!"

And Tiger went, with his tail between his legs.

「もりの　おうさまか。」と　きつねは　わらいました。それから　にやりとして
くすくすと　わらいが　こみあげてきました。そして　いえに　つくまで　ずっと
おおわらい　していたそうです。

"King of the Forest," said Fox to himself with a smile. His smile grew into a grin,
and his grin grew into a giggle, and Fox laughed out loud all the way home.

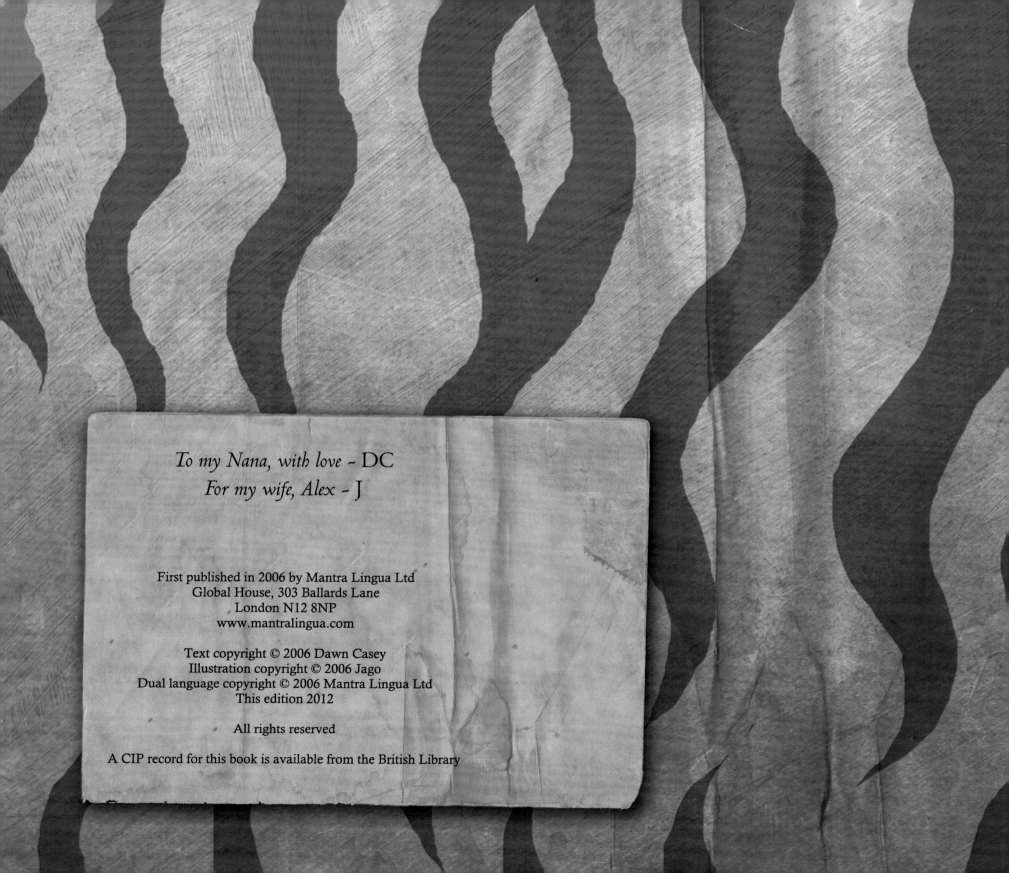

To my Nana, with love - DC
For my wife, Alex - J

First published in 2006 by Mantra Lingua Ltd
Global House, 303 Ballards Lane
London N12 8NP
www.mantralingua.com

Text copyright © 2006 Dawn Casey
Illustration copyright © 2006 Jago
Dual language copyright © 2006 Mantra Lingua Ltd
This edition 2012

A CIP record for this book is available from the British Library